Hooray for Pig!

by CARLA STEVENS

Pictures by RAINEY BENNETT

SCHOLASTIC BOOK SERVICES

NEW YORK · TORONTO · LONDON · AUCKLAND · SYDNEY · TOKYO

ISBN: 0-590-04727-2

Text copyright © 1974 by Carla Stevens. Illustrations copyright © 1974 by Rainey Bennett. All rights reserved. Published by Scholastic Book Services, a division of Scholastic Magazines, Inc.

15 14 13 12 11 10 9 8 7 6 5   01/8

Printed in the U.S.A.

Pig was making two big
peanut butter sandwiches.
He heard a knock on his door.
He opened it, and there
was his friend, Raccoon.

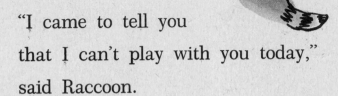

"I came to tell you
that I can't play with you today,"
said Raccoon.

"Why not?" asked Pig.

"Because I'm going swimming
with Muskrat."

"But what about our picnic?"
asked Pig.

"Not today," said Raccoon.
"Maybe tomorrow."

When Raccoon reached the gate,
he turned and said,
"Too bad *you* can't swim."

"Swimming isn't everything,"
said Pig.

Pig sat on his steps.

His feelings hurt a little.

"Some friend," he said to himself.

Then he thought about
the two peanut butter sandwiches.
"A picnic at the lake
is much more fun than swimming.
I'll be there
just in time for lunch."

When Pig got to the lake,
he sat down on the grass
and opened his picnic basket.

"Hi, Pig!"

Pig looked up. There was Otter.

"How about a swim?" asked Otter.

"No, thanks," said Pig.
"I'm having a picnic.
And besides, I don't swim."

"Swimming is *my* favorite sport,"
said Otter. "I do it all the time."

"You do?" asked Pig.

"Sure," said Otter. "Just watch me."

Otter climbed the slide.

WHOOSH!

He slid down into the water and swam
around and around and around.

"It looks easy enough," said Pig.

"It's very easy," Otter said.
"Why don't you try it?"

"I can't," said Pig.
"I'm having a picnic."

"Come on, Pig. The best way to learn
to swim is to get wet. Just try it."

"Oh, all right," said Pig.
He climbed to the top of the slide
and looked down.

"I'm quite high up here," he said.

"I'll count," said Otter.
"One. Two. Three. Go!"

But Pig just stood there,
looking down.

"Come on, Pig. Don't be afraid.
I'll count again.
One. Two. Three. Go!"

But Pig did not move.

"Hey, Pig!" shouted Otter.
"Can't you hear?
ONE. TWO. THREE. GO!"
Still, Pig did not move.

"Hurry up, Pig.
You're holding up the line,"
Beaver said.

"Time for lunch," said Pig.
And he started to back down
the slide steps.

"Hey, you can't do that!"
shouted Beaver. "Get going!"

"Yeah," said Duck, who was behind
Beaver on the slide steps.
"I want my turn."

Suddenly everyone on the slide
began to push.

"Stop pushing! I'm slipping. . . .
Oh help!"

"That wasn't so hard, was it?"
asked Otter. "Now try it again."

"That's the worst,
the very worst thing I ever did
in my whole life," said Pig.
"I almost drowned."

"Don't be silly, Pig," Otter said.
"The water is only up to your knees.
Now, hurry and do it again
before you lose your nerve."

"I've already lost it," said Pig.
"I'm going home."

"Just because Raccoon and Otter
can swim doesn't mean I have to,"
said Pig to himself.
"Not all pigs in the world swim."
And he went inside his house
and closed the door.

The next day was very, very hot.
It was so hot that Pig
didn't feel like doing anything.
He sat in the shade and thought
about how he could cool off.

"Hi, Pig!" There was Otter.
"Swimming lessons are at ten.
Don't be late."

"I can't come," said Pig.

"Why not?"

"I'm too hot."

"The water will cool you off,"
said Otter. "Go get a towel.
I'll wait."
Otter waited.
So Pig went inside
to get a towel.

On the way to the lake, Otter said,
"You're going to have fun today."

"Swimming isn't any fun for me,"
said Pig.

"That's because you're afraid
of the water," said Otter.

At the lake, Otter blew his whistle.
"OK," he said. "Up we go."

"Up?" asked Pig. "Up? Must I?"

"Yes, you must."

Pig slowly climbed the slide steps.

He looked down.

He took a deep breath.

Then he closed his eyes.

SPLASH!

"That's great!" said Otter.

Pig opened his eyes.

"I slipped," he said.

"Now you have to get used to putting your face in the water," said Otter.

"Why?" asked Pig.

"Because when you swim that's what you do. Take a deep breath."

Pig took a deep breath.

He closed his eyes again
and put his face in the water
a tiny, tiny bit.

"You didn't put your face
all the way in," said Otter.
"Do it again and open your eyes."

"What for?" asked Pig.

"You'll see."

Pig opened his eyes in the water.
He saw little fish swimming by.
"It looks so easy,"
he said to himself.

"Blow a few bubbles," said Otter.

Pig blew a few bubbles.

"Now try moving your arms
and kicking your legs like this."

Pig kicked his legs and moved his arms.

He made little splashes.

He made big splashes.

He blew more bubbles.

Then he just sat quietly.

"I'm not hot any more," he said.

The next morning
Pig heard a knock on his door.
He knew who it was.

"All set to go?" asked Otter.

"I still can't swim," said Pig.

"You will soon enough," said Otter.

When they got to the lake,
Otter climbed the slide
and slid into the water.

"What are you waiting for, Pig?"
shouted Otter.

"It's not so hot today," said Pig.
"I think I will wait for a while."

"Oh, come on in, Pig.
The water is great."

Pig climbed the slide steps.
"What if I can't?"
he thought to himself.
He looked down.
"But I *can!*" And Pig gave himself
a little push and slid
right into the water.
"That was fun!" he said out loud.

"Now you are going to float,"
said Otter.

"Oh no," said Pig. "I'll sink."

"Lie back. I'll hold you."

Pig lay on his back in the water.
He looked up and saw a bird fly by.
"Don't let go, Otter," he said.

"Now kick a little," said Otter.

Pig kicked.

"Good!" said Otter.

He let go of Pig for a moment.

Pig kept on kicking.

"You're swimming!" said Otter.

"You're not touching bottom!"

"Oh, help!

I told you not to let go, Otter,"

said Pig.

He stopped swimming

and stood up in the water.

"Is that all there is to it?"
he asked.

"No," said Otter.
"But you've got a good start.
Now you have to practice."

"Thanks for all your help, Otter,"
said Pig.

The next day
there was a knock on Pig's door.

"That must be Otter," Pig said.
But it wasn't Otter. It was Raccoon.

"I came to play with you," he said.

"Where's Muskrat?" asked Pig.

"He's too bossy," said Raccoon.

"I can't play with you today because
I'm going swimming," said Pig.

"Swimming?" said Raccoon.
"You can't swim."

"I'm learning how," said Pig.

"I'll go home and get my mask
and flippers," said Raccoon.

When Raccoon reached the gate,
he called, "Don't forget the lunch!"

Pig smiled. "Some friend!" he said.
And he went inside to make
two peanut butter sandwiches.